The Muppet Babies live in a nursery
in a house on a street that is a lot like yours.
But they can travel anywhere anytime using a special power—
the power of the imagination.
Can you imagine what it would be like to go with them?
Join the Muppet Babies on this adventure and find out.

Weekly Reader Presents

Even Kermit Gets Grouchy

By H.B. Gilmour • Illustrated by Tom Brannon

Muppet Press • New York

One ordinary morning, for no particular reason at all,
Baby Kermit woke up feeling grouchy.

Instead of smiling, he frowned. Instead of being cheerful, he felt cranky. Instead of jumping out of bed eager for a new day to begin, Kermit turned his face to the wall and pulled his blanket up over his head.

"Good morning," Baby Fozzie addressed the frog-shaped lump in Kermit's bed. "I can see you are not your happy-go-lucky self today." Fozzie chuckled. "Or should I say, *hoppy*-go-lucky?"

Kermit groaned.

"Kermie has awakened in a grouchy mood," Baby Piggy observed. "Oh, well. It happens to the best of us. Even to me."

"Let's not disturb him," Rowlf suggested.

Baby Gonzo agreed. "When Camilla is in a foul mood, I leave her alone, and in no time at all, she feels better."

It seemed like a very good idea. So the Babies tiptoed away.

A few minutes later, Kermit peered out from under his blanket. He didn't understand why his friends had left him alone. They were just trying to help, but Kermit felt deserted.

"How would they feel," he grumbled irritably, "if they looked up and found *me* gone?"

"Humph!" Kermit went on. "I'd rather be alone anyway. I'd rather be alone and far, far away from friends who like me only when I wake up grinning from ear to ear!"

Far, far away. It seemed like a very good idea...

Kermit packed his toothbrush and stepped out into the bright daylight. Birds were singing. The trees were green overhead. But Kermit, who was grumbling about his gloomy feelings and thoughtless friends, didn't even notice.

"This isn't a nice day," he declared. "I say it's a yucky day!"

Above him, the leaves on the trees rustled in an
unexpected wind. Clouds formed, and the day turned as
stormy as Kermit's mood. In just a few minutes, it was
pouring rain.

"Hey, do you mind?" chirped a sparrow. "It was a nice
day before you came along!"

"Humph!" Kermit grumbled. "I guess I'm just a wet
blanket."

Soaked to the skin, Kermit trudged on. As he walked, he felt colder and colder inside. His friends had frozen him out—or so he thought.

"Well, eight can play at that game as well as seven," Kermit declared frostily, as he stopped to remove the icicle that had formed on his nose.

Kermit felt like throwing something. He wanted to throw something as far and as hard as he could. So he reached down to pick up a smooth, black stone.

"Do you mind?" yelped a polar bear. "That's my nose you're trying to grab!"

"Humph," Kermit said grumpily. "Another cold shoulder."

Kermit continued on his way.

"Just because I'm not Mr. Nice Frog anymore, nobody wants to have anything to do with me," he muttered. He began to remember what a good pal he'd always been— polite, kind, easy to please.

"And then, just once, I wake up grouchy," Kermit said to himself, "and all my friends leave me!"

Just thinking about it made Kermit angry. It really burned him up. He got hot under the collar. He was steaming mad!

Kermit took out his handkerchief and wiped his
forehead. He was so angry that he felt waves of heat rising
around him. He faced a burning desert. Beyond that was a
mountain. Isolated and majestic, the mountain towered
halfway to the sky. It would be the perfect place to be
alone.

The sand beneath Kermit's feet was as hot as his temper. He hopped from dune to dune as quickly as he could. Suddenly, one of the dunes rose out of the sand.

"Hey! Hop off the hump! O.K.?" a camel hissed, staring hard at Kermit.

"Hump? Humph. I know when I'm not wanted," Kermit replied, hopping away.

The sun was beginning to set as Kermit arrived at the foot of the mountain. Weary and wheezing from his trek across the desert, he began the climb. The desire to be alone kept him going until he reached the peak.

"Alone at last!" shouted Kermit as night fell.

"Not so fast," bleated a bearded old mountain goat. "You happen to be standing in my living room."

"Humph," Kermit declared. "There's obviously not enough living room here for the two of us. I'll just have to find somewhere else to be alone."

Kermit spied a moonbeam traveling up toward the stars. He stepped onto it. Being careful to hold the handrail as Nanny had taught him, he took the moonbeam to the first meteor he found. There, in the stillness of space, he sat on his suitcase, with his back to the world—a little lost frog in the universe, sullen, sighing, and, at last, alone.

After a few minutes, Kermit cleared his throat and did what he had wanted to do all day. He shouted. At the top of his lungs, he hollered out into the silent universe. He stamped his feet and shook his fists. He whined and complained and told the stars how unfair the world was.

"Did that make you feel better?" a voice asked.
Kermit whirled around. He had awakened the moon!
"Well…not really," Kermit replied.
"Lighten up. Have some fun," the moon advised. "It's
the best cure for grouchiness in the entire solar system."

At the moon's suggestion, Kermit took a ride on a comet rollercoaster. He cooled off in a meteor shower. Then he hopped from star to star and made a big splash in the Little Dipper. He began feeling like his old self again.

Kermit turned to thank the moon. But it had already faded. It was the dawn of a new day. It was time to get back to the nursery now. But how? There were no more moonbeams to ride.

Suddenly, the star Kermit was standing on began to move. He spied a pair of leather reins, decorated with tinkling silver bells. He took hold of the reins just as a bright tail of light exploded from the star.

Like a space cowboy standing on the back of a bucking bronco, Kermit held tightly to the reins and rode that shooting star all the way to Earth.

He landed with a thud right back in his own bed. When he sat up, smiling, Fozzie and Piggy wandered over, looking very glad to see him.

"Tell me something," Kermit said to them. "Are you glad to see me just because I'm not grouchy anymore?"

"Of course not," said Fozzie. "We're glad to see you anytime, any way you feel. No kidding."

"Everyone gets grouchy sometimes, Kermie," Piggy pointed out. "Even you!"

That's true.